Can We Get a Dog?

Written by: Nicole Beaulieu
Illustrations: Anselm Medina

"Wow, look! Let's go in to see!
Can we get a dog?"
The boy asked joyfully.

Mom thought about the question hesitantly, "I don't know... Dogs are a BIG responsibility."

"You will need to teach it tricks," Mom said. "That will be fun!" He nodded his head.

Mom continued, "You also feed dogs twice a day."
The boy excitedly shouted, "That's okay!"

Mom explained, "It takes a lot of time to potty train."
He thought, that might be hard but I won't complain.

Mom stated, "To stay healthy,
dogs should be brushed and cleaned."
"No problem!" The boy beamed!

"Most importantly," shared Mom,
"You must love it with your whole heart."
He kindly smiled, "That will be the easy part!"

Secretly, Mom had wanted a dog for a while,
she thought with a big smile.
So they went inside to meet the furry pups.
Two of them came right up!

One small pup was the sweetest!
He stole their hearts;
This adoption would be the greatest!

Teaching the dog was fun.
He learned to sit, stand,
rollover, and run!

The boy fed him every
morning and every night.
It was always such a delight!

He treasured potty walks
with his new best friend.
He never wanted them to end!

Bath time was always a blast
as the dog squirmed and splashed!

The boy and his dog grew up together;
their memories and adventures
are sure to last forever!

Dedicated to all the furry friends
who bring joy and happiness
to their families.

Made in United States
North Haven, CT
26 May 2023

37009613R00015